For Tamar, who inspires me with her own beautiful rock 'n' roll
soul. And for my soulful, musical, talented Sophia, who makes the
world a better place with her song.
—S. V.

For Tamar, who puts a little rock 'n' roll
into every book she makes.
—M.C.

The art in this book was created with pen and ink and watercolor.

Cataloging-in-Publication Data has been applied for
and may be obtained from the Library of Congress.

ISBN 978-1-4197-2849-5

Printed and bound in China
10 9 8 7 6 5 4 3 2 1

Abrams Books for Young Readers are available at special discounts when purchased in quantity for
premiums and promotions as well as fundraising or educational use. Special editions can also be created
to specification. For details, contact specialsales@abramsbooks.com or the address below.

ABRAMS The Art of Books
195 Broadway, New York, NY 10007
abramsbooks.com

ROCK 'N' ROLL SOUL

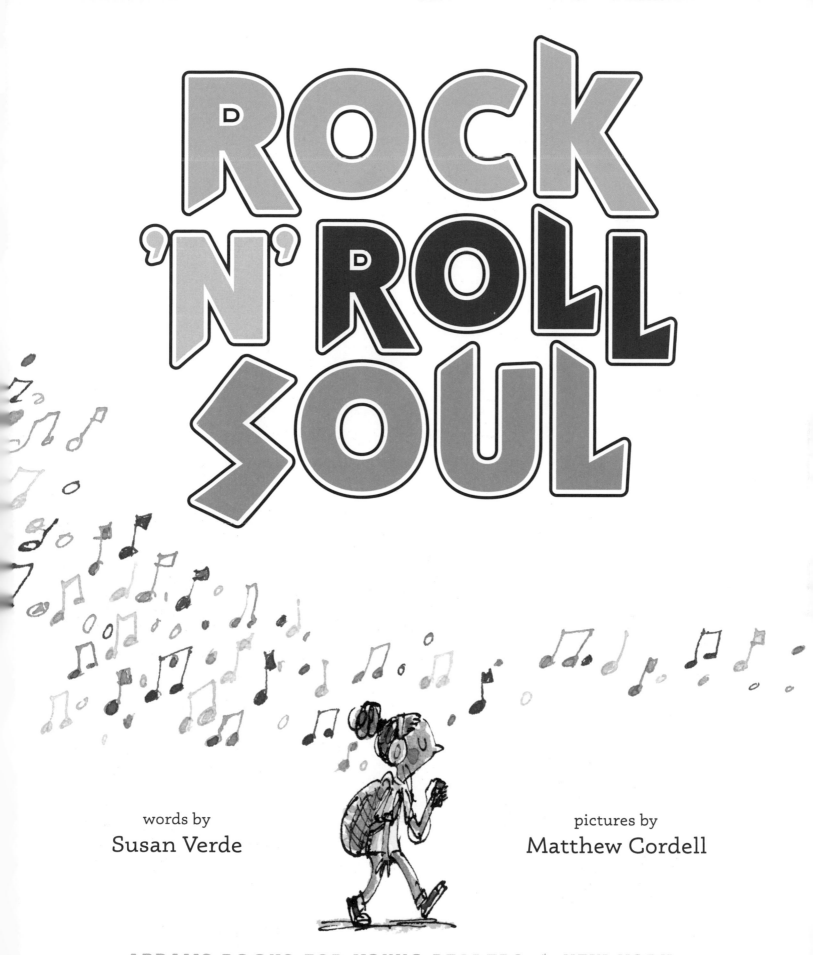

words by
Susan Verde

pictures by
Matthew Cordell

ABRAMS BOOKS FOR YOUNG READERS ♪ NEW YORK

I may not own a drum kit
or an electric guitar.

I might not have a keyboard
or a mic like a rock 'n' roll star.

But I can make the music flow,
I can jam and put on a show.

Only a stick and the city street
are what I need for a thumpin' drumbeat.

Joyful noises fill the air,
fists full of pebbles I shake here and there.

Give me a guitar with just one string.
I can make that one string sing!

All I need to create a tune
is a bowl and a wooden spoon.

When the rain hits my roof, I hear every heavy drop.
I move and I groove and never want to stop.

The smooth rhyme of hip-hop with a kickin' bass
makes my heart pump, jump, and race.

My body simply rises and floats
when I'm a part of those classical notes.

I croon and I swoon when I'm feelin' low down.
I've got a bluesy vibe—it's a smooth, satin sound.

I've got a jazzy swagger, cool to the bone,
slick like a sax or the slide trombone.

I'm electric, magnetic, I can ROCK all the way,
larger than life, center stage as I play.

Keep it down? Keep it quiet?
Oh, I can keep it soft . . .
but the music in my world NEVER shuts off.

High and low like a roller-coaster ride,

I've got music on the out and inside.

I'm a solo piece that I command.

Listen up! I'm a one-girl band.

I...

Here I am!

I've got it all.

There's nothing more I need.

My greatest instrument is . . .

ME.